MAGIC
IN THE
MIST

MAGIC IN THE MIST

Margaret Mary Kimmel

Illustrated by

Trina Schart Hyman

A Margaret K. McElderry Book

Atheneum 1975 New York

Library of Congress Cataloging in Publication Data

Kimmel, Margaret Mary.
Magic in the mist.

"A Margaret K. McElderry book."
SUMMARY: Thomas living in west Wales studies long
and hard to become a wizard but with very little success.
[1. Wales—Fiction. 2. Wizards—Fiction] I. Hyman,
Trina Schart, ill. II. Title.
PZ7.K5649Mag [E] 74-18186
ISBN 0-689-50026-2

Published simultaneously in Canada by
McClelland & Stewart, Ltd.
Manufactured in the United States of America
Printed by The Murray Printing Company
Forge Village, Massachusetts
Bound by A. Horowitz & Son/ Bookbinders
Clifton, New Jersey
First edition

FOR DILYS.
1974 ♡

Once, when mountains sang and people listened, when Cader Idris was covered by snow and Plynlimon was hidden by fog, there lived in west Wales a boy named Thomas. His home was a rude shelter at the edge of a bog, not far from the sea. Thomas was studying to be a wizard. Although he spent long hours with

books, practicing spells and chanting incantations, his magic was not very strong. In fact, it was not even strong enough to keep his house warm. Each morning as the cold wet day began, Thomas would try to light the house fire. In spite of all his spells, the rain kept on dripping into the small hut, the wind blew through chinks in the walls, and Thomas could do no more than strike a weak spark.

Thomas had few visitors in his home, for even the creatures of the bog liked a bit of warmth. He was able to coax only one small toad into the hut to keep him company and Thomas called him Jeremy. Jeremy had lived in the bog for a long time and had learned to listen to the wind. Sometimes, he could even repeat the song it sang. Sometimes, he hummed along when Thomas practiced a new spell.

One blustery day, when Jeremy was listening to the west wind stir the sea, he began to hum a tune he'd made up. Suddenly, the wind, which had been quite fierce, calmed. It was a very unexpected lull—and Jeremy was startled.

"Ych-y-fi," murmured Thomas, who had been sitting quietly, listening to Jeremy and the wind. Now there was no sound at all from outside the house. Inside, both Jeremy and Thomas waited—for what, neither could say.

Quietly, Thomas picked up the toad and peered out of the hut. The world was covered in mist, the bog and the sea beyond as hushed and waiting as the two in the doorway. Drops of rain hung in the air as if falling to the ground would break the expected stillness.

Thomas knew it was a special moment. He took two steps into the silent bog, and then two more…then he froze. Directly ahead, in a clump of marsh grasses, something stirred. It was not a very big thing, but Thomas caught his breath.

Slowly, he stepped closer and closer. The feel of Jeremy's heart thumping steadily as he held him in his hand comforted Thomas. He dropped to his knees and carefully parted the grasses. There, in a nest of reeds and moss, lay one small dragon. In all his days, Thomas had never seen a dragon. He had only heard of them.

Thomas's dragon was a soft spring green in color and obviously very young. The wings were folded along its back and sides, and it trembled as Thomas reached down. Jeremy seemed pleased to see the small dragon and started to hum his tune again. At that very moment, the wind began to breathe once more, the sea to pound, and the rain to fall. Thomas picked up the dragon and carried it with him into the hut. He gave it a bit of fish, all that he had left, and a taste of fresh water.

It was a long day for the three of them. Thomas held Jeremy in one hand and the dragon in the other, as if letting either go might somehow break a spell. Late in the afternoon, he began to long for warmth—a cup of tea perhaps. The dragon was quiet. Jeremy dozed.

There had been no humming since the moment of magic. Moving slowly, so as not to frighten his creatures, Thomas freed his hands and began once again to try lighting the household fire. The scraps of wood seemed even damper than usual. His fire-lighting magic only produced a wisp of smoke and a good deal of wasted breath.

A rustle at his feet caught Thomas's attention. It was the dragon. Thomas watched in amazement as the creature carefully eased its way closer to the pile of sticks. With one graceful breath, a curl of flame from the dragon's mouth kindled the fire for Thomas.

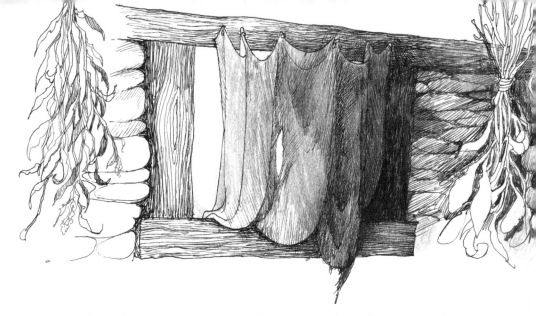

The dragon stayed close to the fire until it burned sturdily. Thomas put on the kettle for his cup of tea and crouched down beside Jeremy to watch the flame. Jeremy began a song, a new song, that echoed the music of the flame and blended with the sound of water bubbling for tea.

There was a moment of listening. Then Thomas whispered, "Please teach me that tune. I want to sing too." The fire grew stronger, warming the hut and those in it.

Sometime during the night, the dragon left, but Thomas and his friend Jeremy are still in their home by the sea. Sometimes other creatures of the bog stop by to listen to their music for now, even when there is no fire, the hut is snug and cheerful. Rain no longer drips in, nor does the wind blow through the walls. Thomas's spells still work only once in a while, but they work best when he and Jeremy share a tune about wind, or flame, or very small dragon wings.

THE END

639999